Also by L.G. Rivera

Dammed

The Blood

Sunk

Short Stories:

Maggie Moo

The Life Coach

Coming Soon

Agobio

Z+

and

The exciting sequel to The Blood:

The Bones

Maggie Moo

L.G. Rivera

Maggie Moo. Copyright © 2010 by L.G. Rivera

All rights reserved under International and Pan-American
Copyright Conventions.
Published in the United States by Studio 223.
Library of Congress Cataloging-in-Publication Data
Rivera, L.G.
Maggie Moo / L.G. Rivera.

ISBN 978-0615456898

Printed in the United States of America

For Susan

"And rounding out the rear in eighth place is Maggie Moo," the loudspeaker blared.

Irving Schwartz looked at his ticket, studying it intently, as if it would change if he stared long enough.

"Crap," he hissed under his breath. He adjusted his black horn-rimmed glasses and looked at the ticket again.

"Crap," he said again. "Well, that's it and that's that," he said to no one. He crumpled the ticket and threw it on the ground.

Irving made his way through the crowd, past the cashiers paying out the winners, to the bar in the back. His skinny wallet came out and he fished for money but there was nothing in it but old creased pictures. Pictures of a life he scarcely remembered, of family long gone. He put the wallet back in his pocket and went up to the bar, not even bothering to get the attention of the bartender. He was invisible anyway.

There was a large bowl of peanuts on the bar. He grabbed a huge handful and stuck them in the pocket of his plaid jacket and walked away.

There he was, he thought, *old Irving Schwartz with the peanuts in the pocket.* He cursed at himself.

Irving walked out of the dog track into the searing Florida August sun.

"No more dogs," Irving said out loud. "No more horses. No steak for dinner tonight."

He walked his long way through the baking asphalt ocean to his car. The flat-brown 1977 Thunderbird, huge and imposing, waited for him. He swung the massive door and sat in it, a small man lost in a sea of car. The merciless sun had long ago faded the paint into an ugly memory of its original color, and that is what he felt like now. Faded. Gone. Forgotten but not quite finished off.

Irving cranked the big car and it roared to life. He aimed the hood ornament's crosshairs at the horizon and drove off to his apartment. He couldn't really call it a home. He had not been home for a very long time.

He drove on. The sun was red like a burning coal on the horizon.

"Old Irving Schwartz with the peanuts in the pockets," he said out loud in the emptiness of the car.

He cursed at himself again and closed his eyes a moment. If he hadn't been driving he would have closed his eyes forever.

"**Y**ou really should get you something," Angie the landlady told Irving a few days later as they stood on the steps of the apartment. "A dog or something. I wouldn't mind. And it'd be good for you."

"What the hell would I want with a dog?" Irving asked. "I ain't never had a dog in my life."

"It'd be good for you," Angie repeated, "keep you company."

"Alright, alright, I'll think about it," Irving said, then paused. "And Angie, thanks for the time on the rent," Irving said earnestly.

Angie waved her hands. "Don't worry about it, hon."

"It's just that I don't get my check till the middle of the month and—"

Angie cut him off. "I said don't worry about it. I know you're good for it. You're a good man," she said and put her hand, all paper-thin skin and wrinkles like his own, on his padded shoulder. She then laughed a good-natured laugh. "Irving, you're the only one I know that wears a jacket in Florida, hon."

Irving stood up a bit straighter and buttoned the plaid jacket.

"I like it. Makes me feel — respectable."

"You don't need a jacket for respect," Angie said.

"Maybe I don't and maybe I do," he said, with mock indignation, and then smiled at her.

"Okay, Okay," Angie put her hands up. "Just think about the dog."

"Alright already, I will," he said.

Irving waved goodbye and walked up the stairs to his one-bedroom apartment. He walked in, past a dusty chessboard sitting on a small table off to the side. He sat on the couch, flipped on the T.V. and watched Judge Judy berate some poor unfortunate defendant. Old yellowed pictures of a son he no longer had and a wife long-gone watched along with him.

Two days later Irving Schwartz walked up and down Citrus Groves mall. There were no citrus and no groves, not anymore, just baking asphalt and the cool artificial dome of the shopping mall. Irving shuffled around, not really shopping, just going from one end of the mall to the other. He had nothing to do and no one to do it with. Coffee was out of the question at four bucks a pop, so Irving sat by the cool of the ice rink and watched the skaters. When he tired of watching little kids slip and fall on the ice, he moved on. The ice reminded him of up north anyway, of Rockefeller Center, of better times, of holidays and families and busy city streets.

"Now there's nothin'," Irving said to himself. "You got no one left old man," he muttered again, shuffling along in his plaid jacket, just another crazy old man talking to himself. A great emptiness seemed to reach out at him, to open a great chasm in front of him.

"Stop it," he said, louder. "Stop feeling sorry for yourself, dammit." After all, he thought to himself, he was alive. Still alive. A lot of good that it was doing him, though.

Irving turned a corner and there were dogs everywhere.

5

"What the hell?" he asked out loud to no one in particular.

There were dogs in cages and dogs on leashes and people milling around. Above it all a large banner hung reading, "ADOPT A DOG."

"Hello sir," a friendly and wrinkled face came up to him while he was staring at the banner. She put a flyer in his hand. "Have you ever considered adopting a dog? Maybe one of our Greyhounds?"

"What?" Irving asked. "What do I want with a dog, and a big dog like that? I ain't ever had a dog."

"Oh, they're great companions," the old lady said. "I've got one myself and I can tell you it's just about the sweetest friend you can have."

Irving shook his head.

"Oh, let me show you at least," the sweet old lady said and motioned to Irving to follow her.

Irving shrugged. "What else I'ma gonna do?" he asked himself and followed after her.

Rows of cages lined with blankets stood on the side against the wall. A little girl stood in front of one open cage, petting a tall Greyhound. She was dwarfed by the big dog. Irving stood still and watched her and watched the dog. The little girl was very blond, with white hair that just about glowed. She patted the dog on the head. The dog, long and lithe and elegant, stood there patiently, its mouth half open and eyes half closed, looking serene and calm.

"Over here," the old lady called out, breaking Irving from his trance. Irving moved on, past the little girl and shuffled over to one of the large cages towards the end.

"This one," the lady said, "this one is a special one. She's such a sweetie."

Irving looked over at the cage. Inside, a white and brown Greyhound lay on a blanket on the floor of the cage, her paws crossed and her head resting forlornly on top of them. She looked up with big liquid brown eyes at the pair of old people before her, but did not move.

"She's a schmoopie-poo this one is," the old lady said.

Irving looked down at the dog and felt something. He did not know what. It was like a tickle inside him, a gentle sad warm thing behind his eyes. The dog looked so sad and lonely, so *deeply* sad.

"What's her name?" Irving asked.

"Maggie Moo," the old lady said, "but you could change it if —"

"Maggie Moo?" Irving interrupted her.

"Yes. Like I said, you could change it if you wanted to."

Irving shook his head and laughed. "Maggie Moo, Maggie Moo," Irving repeated, almost to himself, smiling and shaking his head. "Rounding out the rear, Maggie Moo."

At the sound of her name, the Greyhound stood up and stretched out as much as she could in the cage, arching her back and giving a big yawn.

"So what's her story?" Irving asked. "How'd she get here?"

"Well, most of these Greyhounds were used in the races, and when they're no good to them anymore, when they're too old, a group like ours takes them in, cares for them, finds them a home. Some of the Greyhounds were never even in the races, they were just not good enough for the breeders or injured when young." The old lady leaned down and opened the cage. "They're just the sweetest dogs, you know."

Maggie Moo slipped slowly out of the cage and took two steps to Irving, then craned her neck, putting her head right under Irving's hand, gently nuzzling it.

"See, she likes you," the old lady said.

Despite himself, Irving smiled. A real smile that came from deep inside. He patted the dog's head with a hesitant hand. Maggie Moo gazed up straight into Irving's eyes, her soulful chocolate-brown eyes sweet and sad and understanding everything about Irving in that instant. Irving suddenly felt a tear, then another tear, welling up in his eyes, and he had no idea why.

He heard himself saying, "I'll take her. She's great."

"Wonderful," the old lady said. "I knew you two were perfect for each other. I'll go get the paperwork ready," she said and walked towards a table with other volunteers, leaving them alone for a few moments.

Irving looked down at Maggie Moo, petting her on the head and on her flanks.

"Maggie Moo," Irving repeated to himself. The dog leaned down, raising her rear in the air, wagging her tail playfully. "I lost my bet but I won the dog," Irving said, and laughed and shook his head in disbelief.

Irving signed a dozen papers and got instructions on how to care for her and a free leash and collar and a small bag of dog food. Irving and Maggie Moo made their way out of the mall, everyone staring at the little old man walking the big greyhound through the normally dog-free mall. They walked out and through the long parking lot out to Irving's ancient Thunderbird. The door creaked open and Maggie Moo jumped in and vaulted over the seatback to the backseat. Irving scooted in, belted up, and they were off.

"I don't know where I'm gonna put you yet," Irving said. "I got a little place, but we'll find a place for you."

Irving looked into the rearview mirror and Maggie Moo stared back at him, panting in the heat of the car.

"Yeah it's hot in here," Irving said, adjusting the collar of his jacket. He opened the window. Maggie Moo stuck her head out, tongue flapping wildly in the wind.

They drove like this down palm tree lined avenues and over the bay bridge, with blue green waters sparkling jewel-like in the shining Florida sun.

Irving hardly needed the leash. Maggie Moo stuck to his side like glue, following him from the car to the apartment.

"Good heavens, what is that?" Angie the landlady exclaimed. She was standing outside her door down the hall.

"This is Maggie Moo and she's a she and not a 'what' or a 'that'," Irving said, a trace of protective annoyance in his voice.

"And what are you doing with her?" Angie asked.

"What do you mean what am I doing?" Irving said, "I'm going up to my apartment."

"With her?" Angie asked.

"Yeah with her," Irving said. "You said I should get a dog, so I got a dog."

"Oh, Irving," Angie sighed, "I meant a little dog. Couldn't you get a little dog? Like a poodle or something?"

"I don't like poodles and I don't like dogs. But I like Maggie Moo here," Irving said and patted her on the head. Maggie Moo glanced up at Irving then looked over at Angie with those big liquid brown eyes.

"Well," Angie said, "I suppose I could look the other way. You know the pets aren't supposed to be over thirty-five pounds."

"Look at her," Irving said, "she's skinny as can be. Thirty-five pounds tops."

Angie smiled. "Sure, sure. Just don't have her tear up the place."

"Relax, she's a good dog," Irving said, and turned to Maggie Moo. "Aren't you, girl?"

Maggie Moo wagged her tail and barked once. Angie laughed, and Irving joined her, giving a little chuckle.

"**W**ell, this is it," Irving said, closing the front door behind him. Irving's apartment was cluttered but clean. The kitchen was spotless as he hardly used it. The chessboard he and his wife battled on years ago sat dusty and abandoned on a small table, frozen in mid-match. They walked in.

"We'll just set up a nice little place for you here," Irving said as he brought out blankets and comforters from a closet, old comforters that were his son's from so many years ago. Irving piled them up in a corner of his bedroom. Maggie Moo went over and sniffed them, then wandered over back to the living room.

"What do you want, Maggie?" Irving asked. "You want food?"

Irving brought out the small bag of dog food and poured some into a salad bowl. Maggie gave a little whine and ignored the food.

"Well, what is it?" Irving asked again. "Whaddya want?"

Maggie Moo stared at Irving with big sad brown eyes and gave another high whine. Irving thought.

"A drink! That's what you want, isn't it?" Irving poured some water into another salad bowl.

Maggie lapped it up eagerly and when she was done Irving poured more into the bowl. She then turned and gave Irving a wet sloppy dog kiss on the cheek as he was bent over filling the bowl.

"Okay, Okay," Irving laughed, "so you were thirsty."

That night Irving slept on his bed and Maggie Moo slept on her piled-up blankets and comforters, smelling the long gone family from years ago. To Maggie, they were there with them in the room. Irving's long-dead wife Muriel gazed upon the peaceful scene from her picture on the nightstand, watching them sleeping soundly and wonderfully.

A few days later Irving drove down the road in his huge brown Thunderbird. Maggie Moo sat in the front seat with her long front legs on the floor.

"I haven't been to the park in," Irving paused, "well, I don't remember so it's gotta be a long time." Irving looked over at Maggie Moo. "You'll like it, you'll see."

Maggie Moo looked over at him and almost seemed to smile.

Irving parked the car and walked to the gate of the Dog Park. He went inside the gate, bent down and took Maggie Moo off the leash, but she stayed by his side. Irving went to a bench and sat and Maggie Moo followed right along.

"Go on you, go run!" Irving said. There were big dogs and small dogs of all shapes and sizes, some with nervous guarded owners and others with owners that were just relaxing and enjoying a beautiful warm Florida day.

"Go on," Irving said, and waved his hands.

Maggie Moo turned and walked slowly away, exploring the park, sniffing here and there. She went to a water fountain and lapped up some water. Little dogs would come up to her and she would peer down curiously at them. She walked around, some of the little dogs following her.

Maggie Moo then glanced up and saw a wide-open grassy field and she trotted towards it, then started running, leaping in long graceful strides. Other dogs saw her and started running after her but they could not catch her. She bounded effortlessly across the field from one end of the park to the other. Her tongue hung out of her mouth and she almost seemed to smile as the scenery blurred past her. Maggie ran and ran and Irving looked at her and marveled at her grace and speed.

"That's a good looking dog," said a middle-aged lady that was standing nearby looking at the dogs running. "Is it yours?" she asked.

"She sure is," Irving said, straightening his jacket, and smiling. Maggie Moo ran and ran, and the sun shone down and the grass was green and Irving smiled and felt great, something he hadn't felt in a very long time.

Later, back at the apartment, Irving prepared a nice microwave meal for himself and poured Maggie some of the gravy over her food. After they ate and watched Judge Judy for a bit, Irving yawned and went to the bedroom. Maggie followed and went to her bed of piled-up blankets and comforters.

"You gotta be tired, girl," Irving told Maggie Moo as he settled in for the night. "You were the fastest one out there you know."

Maggie Moo rose from her bedding and came over to the bed, resting her chin right on the edge of the bed. Irving patted her head.

"Yes, you're a good girl," Irving said, and drifted off to wonderful sleep.

Irving bought dog food and extra treats and cut back on his own food. He felt better than he had in years. He took Maggie to the park and on walks under cool blue Florida October skies. Everywhere people stopped and talked to him and told him what a handsome and graceful dog he had. Maggie seemed not to pay attention to any of it, but instead stood by Irvin's side and looked at him occasionally with a deep soulful gaze.

"How's Maggie doing?" Angie the landlady asked as Irving and Maggie came back from a walk. "She's not tearing up the place, is she?"

"She's doing nothing of the sort," Irving said. "She's a perfect lady. The best dog ever. A very conscientious and well-mannered hound. A fine ca—"

"Alright, alright, I believe you," Angie interrupted, then added, "and she *is* a cute dog."

"Yes she is," Irving said, and straightened his jacket.

"You sure look better too, Irving." Angie said.

"It's the walks," Irving said, and paused. "You should get you a dog, Angie," Irving told her and laughed. "It'd be good for you."

Angie smiled and then gave a wide grin. "Go on, you."

Irving went up the stairs, Maggie at his side, and walked up to his small apartment. He put the leash away, grabbed a brush, and brushed Maggie Moo, who stood there with a look of serene contentment. Irving was content too.

After he was done, he straightened up the place for a bit, dusting the top of the T.V. and the bookshelf. When he got to the chessboard, he paused and gave a sad smile. Very gently, one by one, he took each piece off, dusted it and the space underneath, then put it back where it was. When he was done, he looked over at an old yellowed picture of Muriel his wife and smiled at her. He cleaned this too. Maggie Moo came over and nuzzled her head against his hand and he gently patted her head.

"This is the first Christmas present I've bought in a very long time," Irving said to Maggie Moo.

She stood in the middle of the living room in the soft glow of Christmas lights from a tiny foot-tall tree. Irving stood before her in his plaid jacket, holding a poorly wrapped present.

"The first present in a long time," he repeated, "and it's for you."

Irving put the wrapped present on the coffee table in front of Maggie, who stared at it vacantly. She then looked up at Irving.

"Okay, Okay, I'll open it for you," Irving said and tore the wrapping paper he had just wrapped, revealing a large rawhide bone. Maggie Moo sniffed it, tested it with her tongue, then closed her mouth around it and squatted on the ground, chewing it.

"Ahh, you like it. I thought you would," Irving said, and smiled.

Irving shuffled slowly over to the kitchen and picked up another poorly wrapped present.

"I'll be right back," Irving said. Maggie Moo turned to look at him, then went back to her bone.

Irving went downstairs and knocked on Angie's door. A single string of colored lights blinked off and on over the door.

"Oh, hi Irving," Angie said as she opened the door. "How you doing?"

"Good, Angie," Irving said, "real good," and he meant it. "I got you a little something," he said.

"Come in, come in," Angie said and Irving went in.

Angie's apartment smelled like mothballs and Pine-Sol and it was very crowded with hundreds of knick-knacks and porcelain teacups filling every shelf, but it was all very clean. Dozens of little gold and white porcelain angels in all manner of poses filled in every spare bit of shelf.

"Here," Irving said and handed Angie the shoddily wrapped box. "Merry Christmas."

"Why thank you Irving," Angie said, surprised, and took the box and put it on her dining room table. She unwrapped it carefully, even though it was a mess of a wrapping job. She peeled the tape from the corners and was careful not to tear the paper, revealing a cardboard box. She opened the box and took out a teacup and saucer. It was very delicate white and pink porcelain and small red roses ringed the rim.

"Oh Irving, its beautiful."

"I know you collect them," Irving said looking at the glass shelf filled with other teacups.

Angie leaned over and gave Irving a hug.

"I don't have anything for you," Angie said, "but thank you, I love it." She leaned over and hugged him again and then gave him a little kiss on the cheek, and he blushed.

"Don't worry about it. That was present enough," Irving said and smiled, still blushing.

Irving labored back upstairs to his apartment, making his slow way up the stairs. Maggie Moo was waiting for him at the door. She had hidden the bone somewhere and stood there, mouth half open. Irving patted her on the head and she licked his hand once and nuzzled her head against it.

"You're such a good dog," Irving said and sat down on the sofa. Maggie Moo stared back at him with deep brown chocolate pools of eyes. Irving smiled weakly.

"Boy am I tired," Irving said, and exhaled. Maggie craned her head. "All that shopping and the stairs." Irving took in a long breath. "I'll just close my eyes for a bit."

Maggie Moo sat at his feet at the foot of the sofa and crossed her paws and laid her head on them. Irving was asleep for a long time. After a while Maggie rose and put her head in Irving's lap, resting her chin on his thigh. Irving opened his eyes slowly and patted Maggie on the head.

"Is it dinner time already?" Irving asked her. "Just give me a moment." Irving sat for a bit then rose slowly. He shuffled over to the kitchen and poured out a big bowl of food for Maggie and bent down, setting the bowl on the ground. Irving straightened up, and leaned on the counter, taking a few deep breaths.

"I think I got up too fast," Irving said to Maggie. "My head's all swimmy."

Maggie looked up at Irving, then down at her food, then back at Irving. She gave a short high-pitched teakettle whistle. Irving rubbed his temple.

"I'm not too hungry tonight," Irving said. "You go ahead and eat. I think I'm gonna turn in early."

Irving shuffled off to the bedroom and Maggie followed. He took off his plaid jacket, with a few peanuts still in the pocket, and hung it up carefully on a wooden hanger. Irving put on his pajamas and crawled into bed. He looked over at the picture of his wife on the nightstand and gave a weak smile. Maggie Moo went to the side of the bed and rested her head on it. Irving patted her on the head, looking into her infinite liquid brown eyes.

"Good night, Maggie Moo," Irving said, then turned his head to her and added "I love you."

Irving clicked off the light. Maggie licked his hand once, and Irving fell into a peaceful sleep.

Irving woke up on warm green grass. He rose up easily and felt great and young. He looked around, disoriented for a moment, but felt no panic. Marble white buildings and trees with yellow and green leaves surrounded him. Through the trees he saw a large white marble arch and he knew instantly where he was. Back in New York, in Washington Square Park. The air was cool and the sun was warm and he walked, hopping easily over the black chain encircling the grass.

There were people all around and some waved at him. When he looked, he began to recognize some of them. He saw his family and long-gone and forgotten friends. Everyone around him enjoying this glorious and perfect day in the park Irving knew and he suddenly remembered and loved. Old squabbles and arguments were forgotten and people one by one came by towards him. Mona his grandmother and Irving the first, then Irving his father, and now Evelyn his dear mother came by and smiled. Suddenly, Mark his son, his beloved son, who had died of polio so long ago, came running up to him on strong healthy legs and he was seven still and forever. Irving hugged him and picked him up easily and spun him around. Everyone looked different yet the same, young and perfect, and Irving could recognize everyone because he could see their souls.

And now Muriel, his long-deceased wife, came to him and she was wedding-day-beautiful and she smiled at him and he cried, but they were tears of joy. Muriel tenderly wiped away every tear. Irving set Mark on the ground, holding his hand. Mark hugged his mom's leg with his other arm.

"Welcome home," Muriel said and hugged Irving and he hugged her back. She was warm and smelled like heaven. He hugged her as if he would never let her go and kissed her neck and cried joyously.

Then Maggie Moo trotted up from the grass, leapt over the chain and came right up to Irving, nuzzling her head in Irving's hands.

"Maggie!" Irving exclaimed. "Maggie girl!" Then he turned to Muriel. "Did Maggie, you know – die too? I mean, that's it right? I'm dead. Right?"

"There's no past and no future here," Muriel said. "Just everlasting present." She breathed in and the light of the sun illuminated her and she looked angelic. "And it is wonderful," she continued. "It is Glory." She closed her eyes and drank in the light.

Irving smiled and hugged Muriel again. He bent down easily and without pain and petted Maggie, who wagged her tail.

Irving took Muriel's hand and Mark's hand and they walked towards the people all gathered under the arch. Old friends, new friends, family, everyone Irving had ever loved. Even Angie was there, who turned to him and smiled.

The wind gently rustled the leaves of the trees and some of them floated like gold leaf to the ground, covering the sidewalks. Over them, a flock of white doves circled around. Irving watched them circle around three times then spiral up to infinite blue heaven skies.

— EPILOGUE —

Maggie barked and barked and barked and finally Angie came up the stairs. She knocked on Irving's door but he did not answer. She fished out her master key and opened the door.

"Irving?" she asked, peeking her head inside.

Maggie Moo stood in the middle of the living room and gave a high-pitched teakettle whistle whine. Angie stepped inside.

"Irving?" she called out again, and again he didn't answer.

Maggie Moo gave one short bark, startling Angie, then walked into the bedroom. Cautiously, Angie walked through the living room and followed Maggie Moo into the bedroom.

Later, after the ambulance and the coroner and the police had left and the flashing of blue and red lights no longer illuminated the apartments, Angie sat on the steps with Maggie Moo, looking into her deep brown eyes.

"I'm so sorry, girl," Angie said. "He seemed so happy and alive." Angie sighed. "I guess it was just his time."

Maggie put her head down and nuzzled Angie's hand.

"Oh, don't you worry girl," Angie said. "I've been thinking about getting a dog, and you're not a little dog but you're a good dog." Angie patted Maggie Moo on the head. "You're about thirty-five pounds, right? No? Well, I guess I can let it slide. Just don't tell the other tenants."

Maggie Moo licked Angie's hand and lay down at her feet at the bottom of the stairs. Angie reached down and patted Maggie's head. She stared out into the oncoming night and sat there on the stairs for a while.

The moon was rising and the dark had just started to drive the day away, and now stars came out to keep light kindled through the long night.

L.G. RIVERA

MAGGIE MOO

L.G. Rivera was born in Spain and loves to travel. From the top of the Eiffel Tower to the impoverished slums of Haiti, he finds beauty and darkness anywhere he goes. He lives in Florida and is the author of three novels and multiple short stories. His next novel, Z+, a zombie tale like you've never read, is scheduled for release in late 2012. You can find more information at www.lgrivera.com.

L.G. RIVERA

Praise for The Blood:

"This is a real page turner, a wonderful story with great action,
plus a travelogue of Europe. Impressive!"

"Welcome, Mr. L.G. Rivera, to my list of 'must-read' authors."

"The book is fast-paced and takes you from horror to romance
to adrenaline-pumping action with mastery. I was also
surprised by the thorough research as well as the
very relatable characters found on every page."

"I really enjoyed reading 'The Blood' and I would recommend
it to anyone who likes a historically-based
great adventure story."